Rain

Rain

WRITTEN AND ILLUSTRATED BY
MANYA STOJIC

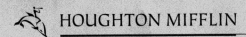 HOUGHTON MIFFLIN   BOSTON

It was hot.
Everything was hot and dry.

The red soil was hot and dry and cracked.

3

A porcupine sniffed around. "It's time," she whispered. "The rain is coming! I can **smell** it. I must tell the **zebras.**"

"Porcupine can smell it. We can **see** it. We must tell the **baboons**."

Thunder
boomed.

"The rain is coming!" cried the baboons.

"Porcupine can smell it. The zebras can see it.

We can **hear** it. We must tell the **rhino**."

A raindrop **splashed.**
"The rain is here!"
said the rhino.

"Porcupine smelled it.
The zebras saw it.
The baboons heard it.

And I **felt** it. I must tell the **lion.**"

The lion
spoke
in a
deep
purr.

"Yes, the rain is here.

I can smell it.
I can see it.
I can hear it.
I can feel it.

And," he sighed,

"I can **taste** it."

It rained

and it

rained

and it

rained.

It rained until every river gushed and gurgled. It rained until every water hole was full.

Then the rain stopped and everywhere long, feathery grasses grew from the soil.

Every tree began to sprout fresh, green leaves.

17

"I can't taste
the rain now,"
purred the lion,

"but I can enjoy
the shade of these

big, green
leaves."

"I can't feel the rain now," said the rhino,

"but I can lie in the **cool, soft, squelchy mud.**"

"We can't hear the rain now," shouted the baboons,

"but we can eat **fresh, juicy fruit** from the trees."

"We can't see
the rain now,"
said the zebras,

"but we can have
a **refreshing
drink** from
the water hole."

"I can't smell the rain now," whispered the porcupine, "but **I know** that it will come back again, when it's **time**."

The sun shone over the plain.

It was **hot.** Everything was drying out.

The red soil was hot and dry.

A tiny crack appeared.